NOBLE SCHOOL

THE MORGAN BAY MYSTERIES

THE MYSTERY OF MORGAN CASTLE

THE MYSTERY OF THE MARBLE ANGEL

THE MYSTERY OF THE MIDNIGHT VISITOR

THE MYSTERY OF THE MISSING MARLIN

THE MYSTERY OF THE MUSICAL GHOST

THE MYSTERY OF MONKS' ISLAND

THE MYSTERY OF THE MARAUDER'S GOLD

THE MYSTERY OF THE MYRMIDON'S JOURNEY

The Mystery

Bill   Lonnie Martin

Illustrations by JOSEPH MANISCALCO

of

Monks' Island

JOHN and NANCY RAMBEAU

Vinny

Gabby

Dave Ballard

FIELD EDUCATIONAL PUBLICATIONS, INCORPORATED
A Subsidiary of Field Enterprises, Incorporated
San Francisco   Palatine, Illinois   Berkeley Heights, New Jersey   Atlanta   Dallas

TABLE OF CONTENTS

THE BOY WITH THE SWITCHBLADE 1

SEARCH FOR AN ISLAND 11

DEAD END 22

OF RUINS AND SHADOWS 36

AN EMPTY POCKET 46

CAUGHT! 56

THUNDER OVER THE MONASTERY 69

THE GHOST TALKS 79

Chapter One

THE BOY WITH THE SWITCHBLADE

Gabby Summers ran down the block, through the gate, and up the front walk. He covered the porch steps in two long jumps and went into the house, letting the door slam behind him.

Bill and Vinny, his older brother and sister, were waiting for him in the living room.

"Well!" Vinny said. "It's a good thing Mother and Dad are away. You would really get it for coming home at this hour."

"You were supposed to be in before dark," Bill said. "It's been dark for an hour. Just where have you been?"

"At the dump, shooting my slingshot," Gabby said calmly. "That's where I said I was going, didn't I? Say, do you want to see this?"

He pulled something out of his pocket and handed it to Bill, who stared at it in alarm.

"What's that thing?" Vinny asked, puzzled.

1

"Good night, it's a switchblade! A switchblade knife," Bill said. "These things are deadly, Gabby. Don't you know it's wrong to carry one of these? You can get in trouble with the police."

"The knife doesn't work, Bill," Gabby said calmly. "See? It's broken."

"Do you mean to tell me you found that knife out at the dump?" his sister asked.

"Well, I didn't really find it," answered Gabby. "A guy gave me the switchblade knife. I gave him my slingshot and ball bearings."

"*What guy?*" Vinny and Bill both said together.

"Oh, a guy who is staying at the dump. Lonnie Martin. You wouldn't know him," Gabby said. "He is new around here. He said that where he came from there was a club called the Shadows. And all the Shadows owned switchblades."

Seeing the look on Bill's face, Gabby asked, "What's wrong with that?"

Bill shook his head. "I don't like the sound of this. Suppose you tell us a little more about Lonnie Martin," he said.

2

"Oh, Lonnie is a good guy—a little different, maybe. He's older than I am, but not as old as you, Bill. He has been all over the country, working in different places. He's staying in a box at the dump until he finds some more work."

"Living in a box!" Bill said.

"Oh, no! What kind of a life is that?" his sister asked. "He must have been kidding you, Gabby."

"He was not kidding. Really! He needed the slingshot and ball bearings to shoot something to eat. That's why he gave up the switchblade knife," Gabby said.

"There isn't anything to shoot at the dump but rats," Bill said. "And he can't eat rats!"

"Mmmm. I was wondering about that, too," Gabby nodded. "Do you suppose it would be all right if I took some sandwiches out to Lonnie tomorrow?"

"Tomorrow!" Vinny cried in alarm. "What's he going to eat tonight? Why don't you boys go out to the dump and bring Lonnie back to the house? He can eat dinner with us. Then we can decide what to do next."

"You want Lonnie to come here?" Gabby frowned. "We-ell, I have an idea that he likes being on his own. I'm not sure . . ."

"Let's try," Bill broke in, pulling Gabby from his chair. "You look for the flashlight, and I'll get my jacket."

Standing in front of the Summers' house was an old hearse. Bill and a friend of his owned it together.

Bill and Gabby climbed into the hearse and drove through the town of Morgan Bay. At the end of town they turned off on the old Jethro Road. A few miles later they turned again and followed a little dirt road that led to the dump.

Leaving the hearse at the side of the road, they turned on the flashlight and started walking. In the beam of the flashlight lay piles of old cans and broken boards.

"There's Lonnie's box," Gabby said. "Lo-n-n-i-e," he called out to his friend.

4

There was no answer.

"He's not inside," Bill said, pointing the flashlight into the box. "I don't see anyone around. Are you sure this is the right box?"

Gabby nodded. "Sure. See, there is his blanket rolled up in the corner. Lonnie must be around here somewhere."

Then Gabby called across the dump once again. "Lonnie! Lonnie, where are you?"

Bill jumped suddenly as something small hit his hand.

"What was that? Say, someone is shooting ball bearings at us."

All of a sudden a rain of ball bearings hit the empty box beside them. Bill turned off the flashlight and ducked behind the box, pulling Gabby after him.

"Lonnie, put down the slingshot, will you?" Gabby called. "It's me . . ."

"I know it's you," came an angry voice from the dark. "I'll teach you to rat on old Lonnie!"

Another ball bearing hit the box.

"What's wrong with him?" Bill whispered.

5

"I told you he was a little different," Gabby whispered back. Then he called out to Lonnie, "I didn't rat on you. We just wanted to ask you to come and eat at our house."

For a long time there was no answer. Finally Lonnie asked, "Who is that with you?"

"It's my brother Bill. Well, are you coming or not?"

Again there was no answer.

Bill sighed. "I guess you were right, Gabby. He doesn't want to come. I suppose we might as well go home."

They slipped out from behind the box. Bill turned on the flashlight, and they started walking toward the hearse. Suddenly they heard Lonnie calling.

"Well, wait a minute, can't you? I have to get my things, don't I? I can't even see where I'm going."

Bill turned and pointed the light across the dump. In its beam they saw Lonnie, picking his way over the piles of cans and broken boards.

"What about your folks?" he asked when he caught up with the two boys. "I mean—man, I don't look so good. What are they going to say?"

8

"Our folks are away," Bill told him. "It's all right for you to come to our place. If you want to, that is."

"Oh. Well, thanks," Lonnie said, climbing into the hearse. "Thanks a lot. I'm sorry I called you a rat and shot at you. I didn't mean to hurt you."

When they reached the Summers' house, Gabby took Lonnie up to his room.

"Put your things in here," he said. "You can wash your hands at the end of the hall if you want to. Then come on down to the kitchen."

"Would it—I mean, would it be all right if I took a shower?" Lonnie wanted to know.

"Of course," Gabby told him. "Why don't you let me put your clothes in the wash? You can wear some of ours until yours are dry."

Leaving Lonnie to shower and change, Gabby took the clothes to wash. Then he helped Bill with the table. Vinny was cooking fish for dinner.

"What do you think of Lonnie?" Gabby whispered to his brother.

"I'll say one thing for him. He's sharp with a sling-shot," Bill answered.

9

Just then Lonnie came into the kitchen. His time in the shower had been well spent. His long, light hair was carefully brushed in a line, covering his eyebrows.

"Man, I really like this house," he said, looking slowly around the kitchen. "It's like the place I lived in when I was little, before my mom died. And that sure looks like a good dinner."

Vinny smiled her thanks and told the boys to start eating. Puzzled, she saw that Lonnie only stared at his dinner, frowning.

"What's wrong, Lonnie?" she asked. "Don't you like fish?"

"Oh, sure. Sure I like it. Only, I guess I should tell you something. I mean, I wouldn't want to get you into trouble or anything," Lonnie said.

"Trouble?" said Bill, looking up quickly. "What makes you think we're going to get into trouble?"

"W-e-l-l," Lonnie said with a sigh, "the police might be looking for me."

Chapter Two

SEARCH FOR AN ISLAND

Vinny and Bill looked at each other in alarm.

"The police!" Gabby said. "How come they are after you, Lonnie?"

"Oh, I didn't do anything really wrong," Lonnie said quickly. "I mean, I just ran away from the Home. But the police might be trying to find me."

"What kind of a home did you run away from?" Bill asked.

"Oh, just a place where you are put if you don't have any folks. My dad died before I was born. He was a flyer in the Korean War, and he was shot down. Then my mother died when I was little. After that I lived at the Home or with different folks that would take me.

"Only, when you're older, as I am, people don't want to keep you. You know, they like little kids better. Finally, I just decided to leave the Home. Besides," Lonnie finished, "there is something I have to find. An island."

"You mean just any island?" Gabby asked.

"No," said Lonnie, frowning.

"Well, what's the name of the island you're looking for?" Bill wanted to know.

"I don't know the name of it," Lonnie answered sharply. "Just forget it! I should never have said anything about it. It was only a wild idea I had."

"But, Lonnie," Vinny said, "if it's near here, we might be able to help you find it. There are some islands just a few miles from Morgan Bay."

"There are?" Lonnie said, his eyes lighting with interest.

Vinny nodded. "You can see them from here on a clear day. Come on, finish your dinner, and we'll go into the living room. We can talk beside the fire. Then you can tell us what you do know about this island."

Settled in a chair by the fire, Lonnie began.

"Mom didn't know much about my dad's folks. I guess she and Dad didn't know each other very long

12

before they were married. And soon after they married, he was sent to the war in Korea.

"The next thing Mom heard was that he had been shot down. She never did believe he was dead. She kept telling me, 'When your father comes home, he's going to take us to live on an island. He's going to teach you to fish and take you exploring. And you can have a horse, just as your father had when he was young.'

"Man, I remember every word," Lonnie said with a sigh. "My mom must have told me that about ten hundred times. I used to dream about that island all the time."

"Is that all she told you?" Bill asked. "Didn't she tell you where the island was?"

Lonnie shook his head slowly. "But when Dad left for Korea, he passed over the island. He looked down and saw his horse, standing in the field. That was in his last letter to Mom. She kept the letter and gave it to me."

Bill reached into the desk behind him and pulled out a map. Opening it on the floor, he studied it.

13

"Look at this map, Lonnie," he said. "Your dad's island might be in this part of the country. There is a flight base about a hundred miles from here. If he left from that base, he might have passed over the islands near here."

"I suppose so," Lonnie said, looking closely at the map. "But shoot! There must be a hundred islands he could have passed."

"Sure there are," Bill told him. "But as long as you're here, why not check out the ones near Morgan Bay? You have to start somewhere."

"What more do you know about your dad, Lonnie?" Vinny asked. "I mean, besides that he was a flyer and lived on an island?"

"Well, his name was Kenneth Martin," Lonnie said. "He died in 1951, the year I was born. That's about all. But—I do have a picture of him. Do you want to see it?"

Lonnie went up to Gabby's room where he had left his things.

"Oh, Bill, I don't think there is any hope," Vinny whispered.

16

"Maybe," said Bill. "But we can't let the boy be picked up by the police and sent back to that Home. We have to keep him here until Mother and Dad get back."

"Do you think they could find a place for him to live in Morgan Bay?" Gabby whispered.

"Maybe," Bill said. "But I'm afraid Lonnie won't stay around very long if he doesn't want to."

Vinny nodded. "We had better keep him looking for that island. Shhh! Here he comes."

Lonnie returned with the photograph and handed it to Vinny. She studied it for a moment.

"I can understand why your mother married Kenneth Martin," she said, smiling. "What a kind face! But he looks so young, Lonnie. This picture must have been taken before he became a flyer."

Vinny turned over the photograph. "Look, Bill. Here is the name of the photographer—'Mark Cousins.' "

"There's a photographer in Jethro named Cousins," Bill said. "He takes pictures for all the high schools."

Vinny looked at Kenneth Martin's face again. "This might have been a school picture. Maybe it was taken when Lonnie's dad graduated from high school. You don't suppose he went to school in Jethro, do you?"

"Search me! Where is Jethro?" Lonnie asked. "Is it on an island?"

Bill shook his head. "It's a small town in the valley about ten miles from Morgan Bay."

"I figured it out!" Gabby cried suddenly, jumping up from his chair. "I'm a genius! I don't think there was any high school on that island where Lonnie's dad lived. It would have taken too long to go to school by boat. So he must have been sent to boarding school. And the only boarding school around here is in Jethro."

"That's right—the Jethro Academy," Bill said. "We may be able to find out something about Kenneth Martin right over the hill in Jethro."

The next day the four piled into the hearse and drove to Jethro. They found the photographer's place Bill had remembered. But though Cousins' name was still on the door, he had moved away.

"Mr. Cousins left town," the new photographer told them. "I dumped out all of his old things. Not a picture is left. Sorry."

Their next stop was the Jethro Academy. School was out, and the halls were empty. Doctor Cook, the head of the academy, was working at his desk. From a high window the light beamed through the blinds down on his white hair.

Bill told him why they had come.

"Kenneth Martin?" Doctor Cook asked, looking at Lonnie. "What year did he graduate?"

Seeing that Lonnie couldn't find his voice, Vinny answered. "We don't know. But it must have been after 1940 and before 1951."

Doctor Cook reached into his desk and pulled out a book. "Hmmm. I don't find Kenneth Martin's name in this book," he said when he had finished looking through it. "These are the names of all of our graduates for those years."

"Maybe he didn't graduate. Maybe he dropped out," Gabby said.

Vinny gave her brother a sharp look.

19

Doctor Cook smiled and said, "We have never had a boy drop out of the academy. Sometimes a teacher drops out, though. Those teachers who can't make their courses interesting don't last long here."

Lonnie had taken the picture of his father out of his pocket. He started to give it to Bill.

"Is that a photograph of Kenneth Martin?" Doctor Cook asked, turning to Lonnie. "May I see it? He might be in our book by another name. That sometimes happens."

Lonnie handed the picture across the desk and watched Doctor Cook study it.

At last Doctor Cook returned the photograph. "I can't tell for sure," he said. "I seem to remember the face. But I don't believe this boy went to the academy. I could be wrong, of course."

"You see hundreds of boys," Lonnie said, finally finding his voice. "I guess you could forget one, couldn't you?"

"I sometimes forget a name," Doctor Cook said. "I never forget a face, though I suppose it could happen. I'm not being of much help to you, am I? I'm sorry."

"Well, thanks for giving us your time," Bill said. "We had better be getting along."

Doctor Cook shook hands with each of them as they left. "I hope you find what you are looking for," he said to Lonnie.

Climbing into the hearse, Lonnie slammed the door and turned to Gabby. "So now we know where my dad didn't go to school. What now, genius? Any more sharp ideas?"

21

Chapter Three

DEAD END

No one talked on the way back to Morgan Bay. If Gabby had any more ideas, he didn't say so. Lonnie sat in a corner of the hearse, staring out of the window.

"Look, we're only getting started," Bill said finally. "Surely, Lonnie, you're not going to give up so soon."

Lonnie didn't answer.

"Let's forget Jethro for the time being . . ." Vinny began.

"I'm for that," Lonnie broke in. "Man, let's just forget all of it. I told you it was a wild idea."

"I thought so, too, last night," Vinny said. "But Mr. Cousins still could have been the photographer who took that picture. And Doctor Cook did seem to remember seeing your father. I don't think our search is over at all. Why, I'm just starting to get excited about it."

"Let's check out the islands," Bill said. "Maybe Mr. Ballard can help us."

"Dave Ballard? The biology teacher at the high school?" Vinny asked.

Bill nodded. "He goes skin diving at the islands a lot. He's interested in marine biology, you know."

"Marine what?" Lonnie asked, brushing the hair out of his eyes.

"Marine biology. That's the study of sea life," said Bill. "Mr. Ballard knows those islands like the back of his hand."

At Dave Ballard's house they were told he was working on his boat, the *Manatee*. The *Manatee*, Bill knew, was tied up at Morgan's Landing.

"The Morgans started this town way before our folks were born," Gabby told Lonnie. "The big house they built is still down beside the bay. It was empty for years and finally was turned into a club. A lot of people keep boats there now."

In a few minutes the hearse pulled through a wide gate and stopped beside some trees. Lonnie followed the Summers as they hurried to the boat landing.

Dave Ballard was washing down the sides of the *Manatee*. He looked up and smiled.

23

"Come on board," he said. "I need a break. How about having some coffee with me?"

Mr. Ballard shook hands with Lonnie. "Happy to know you, Lonnie," he said. "What can I do for you kids?"

"We were wondering if you could tell us a little about the islands," Bill said. "I know you have spent a lot of time skin diving out there."

"That's right. Wait. I'll get my map." Dave Ballard stepped inside the boat and picked up a big map. He rolled it out for them all to see.

"Well, of course, you know about Box Island. That's the big one with the hotel and all the summer homes on it. It's about an hour and half from here," Ballard said. "The other two islands are Table Rock and Monks'."

"Has anyone lived on Table Rock Island?" Vinny wanted to know.

"Oh, yes. A Coast Guard base has been on Table Rock for years. But the Coast Guard won't let you near the place."

"So that leaves Monks' Island," Bill said. "Isn't

that the closest to Morgan Bay—the one we can see from here?"

Dave Ballard nodded. "Why this sudden interest in the islands?" he asked.

Lonnie frowned at Bill. Clearly, he didn't want to tell Mr. Ballard why they were really interested in the islands.

Seeing the look, Vinny put in quickly, "We just wanted something different to do. We thought we might like to try a day exploring."

"There's nothing very interesting to see on Monks' Island," Ballard answered, rolling up the map. "If you're looking for something new, why not go to Box Island? Or let me teach you how to skin dive? Say, I have to finish my coffee and get back to work."

Leaving the *Manatee*, the four of them walked slowly along the landing.

27

"Well, for a teacher he was not much help," Lonnie said. "Man, we're just running into one dead end after another."

"Oh, I don't know, Lonnie. We found out this much," Bill said. "We can cross off Box and Table Rock islands. I would like to know more about Monks' Island, though. I wonder if the Coast Guard could tell us anything."

"Say! What about Lucy Wellington?" Vinny said, an excited light in her eyes. "She has lived here longer than Dave Ballard has. She would know if anyone had lived on Monks' Island. Come on, let's run over and see her."

Vinny jumped from the landing and ran across the beach, the boys following. The old Wellington house stood behind the sea wall, facing the bay. Their old friend Miss Lucy was happy to tell them all she knew. And what she had to tell was quite different from what Dave Ballard had said!

"I should think Monks' Island would be a very interesting place," she said. "I understand there were many Indians on the island at one time. Then, in the late 1700's, some monks settled there and built a small monastery. But in the 1800's the Indians drove the monks away.

"A few years later the Indians left, too. No one knows why. It's said that the island finally became a base for smugglers. They would hold their contraband there until they could move it. But no one really knows for sure.

"For the next few years or so," Miss Lucy went on, "Monks' Island was empty, and the monastery fell into ruins. Then a Frenchman settled on it and built a home there. He lived just as he had in the old country. He built a big house and a barn made of stone. I've never seen it, of course, but I've heard a lot about it. Two sons were born there. One of my school friends married Justin Martineau, one of the Frenchman's sons. Her name was Joanna." ·

"Do the Frenchman's sons still own Monks' Island?" Bill asked. "Do any of them still live there?"

"I don't know, really," Miss Wellington answered. "It was years ago when I knew Joanna. I never heard from her after she married and moved to the island.

She and Justin had a son. But Joanna died when the boy was ten years old."

"What became of the boy and of Justin Martineau?" Vinny asked.

Miss Lucy frowned, trying to remember. "Justin used to come to Morgan Bay quite a lot. But I have not seen his boat at Morgan's Landing for—oh my, I don't know how long. I suppose he has passed away. I don't know what became of his son.

"If you are interested in knowing more, why don't you talk to May White? She stayed with Joanna before she died. She knew the Martineaus very well. She is quite old now. But I believe she still lives at the Bay Manor Hotel."

The Summers thanked Miss Lucy for her help. After leaving the Wellington house, the four of them stood for a moment looking over the sea wall. Across the bay, they could see the dark shadow that was Monks' Island.

"I thought you said that Mr. Ballard knew all about the islands," Lonnie said. "How come he didn't tell us about the Indians, the monastery, and the Frenchman?"

"I'm wondering the same thing," Bill said, puzzled.

"Maybe he's just more interested in marine biology than in Indians," put in Vinny.

"I don't know about that," Gabby said. "He brushed us off the minute we started asking about Monks' Island. Remember?"

"Why don't we go back to the landing and see if we can get a boat?" Bill said. "I would like to see that island, wouldn't you, Lonnie?"

Lonnie brushed the hair out of his eyes and stared across the bay. "Maybe," he answered slowly. "Only I don't see how that Frenchman Martineau could have anything to do with my dad."

"You boys see about the boat," Vinny said. "I'll see you at the house in an hour. Lonnie, I'm going to talk to May White at the Bay Manor Hotel. Will you let me take that photograph?"

"Well—all right. But be careful with it!" he said.

31

The boys climbed over the sea wall. Vinny hurried up the hill toward town. At the desk of the Bay Manor Hotel she asked for Miss May White's room. It was room ten at the end of a long hall.

"Come in," a voice said in answer to Vinny's call.

The room was small and dark. Miss White sat in a rocking chair near a little window. The blinds were down, blocking out the light.

Vinny gave her name and said that she was a friend of Miss Wellington's.

"She thought you might be able to tell me a little about Justin Martineau's son. Do you know where he is now?"

"Paul Martineau?" May White said slowly. "Many times I've wondered what became of that boy. I liked Paul very much."

"Miss Wellington said you were with his mother before she died," Vinny said.

"Joanna Martineau. Yes. That was many years ago. Paul was about ten when she died. He went to boarding school, of course . . ."

"To the Jethro Academy?" Vinny asked.

May White nodded. "Yes, and he spent his summers with his father. But Monks' Island was much too calm a place for that young man! Paul couldn't wait to graduate from school and leave home. My, he had exciting dreams. He wanted to be a flyer."

Vinny caught her breath. "And—and was he?"

"I really don't know. He may have been one," Miss White said. "I remember that Paul's father was so against the idea. Finally, Paul ran away. He came to see me, saying he was never going back to Monks' Island. Where he went, I don't know. I never heard from him again."

Vinny took out the picture of Kenneth Martin. She started to hand it to May White. "Is this—could this be a photograph of Paul Martineau?"

May White shook her head and turned away. "I'm sorry, Miss Summers, I couldn't tell you anything about a photograph. I am quite blind. Didn't you know?"

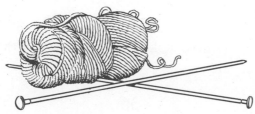

Chapter Four

OF RUINS AND SHADOWS

Vinny was close to crying when she left the Bay Manor Hotel. She didn't quite know if she wanted to cry for May White or for Lonnie Martin. An hour before, she had seemed close to finding out something about Kenneth Martin. Now there seemed to be no answers to the puzzle.

Walking up the hill toward home, she dried her eyes. She didn't want Lonnie to see her long face. Hope was the only thing she and the boys had to give Lonnie. Vinny didn't want to be the one to take that hope away.

The hearse was standing in front of the house. The boys were back from the club. On the hall table, Vinny saw the jacket Lonnie had been wearing. She slipped the photograph into the pocket of the jacket and closed the zipper.

In the kitchen the boys were at the table, eating sandwiches. Lonnie asked at once about Miss May White.

"Oh, Lonnie, May White is blind. She couldn't even see the photograph." Vinny told them all that had happened at the Bay Manor.

"I still don't see how Paul Martineau and my dad could be the same man," Lonnie said. "Mom said that my dad liked his island. Man, he couldn't wait to take us there. Now, that doesn't sound like Paul Martineau to me."

Bill sighed. "People change, Lonnie. I wouldn't give up the idea so soon."

"What about Monks' Island?" Vinny asked. "Were you able to get a boat?"

"Mr. Ballard is going to take us," Gabby said.

"Mr. Ballard!" Vinny's eyes opened wide.

"That gave me a start, too," Bill said. "He heard us talking to some of the boys at the landing. He said he had not told us about the monastery because he didn't think we would be interested. He said he would be happy to show us the ruins if we wanted to see them."

"We asked Mr. Ballard about a house on Monks' Island," Gabby said. "He thinks Miss Lucy was talking about a house on Box Island."

"I don't understand Mr. Ballard," Lonnie said, putting down his sandwich.

"Dave Ballard is tops as a teacher," Bill said quickly. "He is well thought of in Morgan Bay."

"I just said I don't *understand* him," Lonnie shot back. "What's wrong with that? One minute the guy doesn't want to talk about Monks' Island; the next minute he can't wait to take us there."

"We don't have to go if you don't want to, Lonnie," Vinny said calmly.

Lonnie stared at her over his sandwich. "Don't get me wrong," he said finally. "I like Mr. Ballard. You don't have to understand someone before you can like him, you know. You have to *like* him before you can understand him—or even want to!"

The next day the Summers and Lonnie were waiting at Morgan's Landing. Very soon they saw Dave Ballard hurrying toward them.

"Brrr, it's freezing," he said. "I hope you have some coffee in that basket, Vinny. Come on, let's climb on board and get started."

The *Manatee* pulled away from the boat landing and started across the bay toward the dark island.

"Sorry to get you out here at this hour," Mr. Ballard told them. "I telephoned the Coast Guard yesterday. They said there might be showers later on. You know the bay can get wild in a storm."

In little more than half an hour they came to Monks' Island. The island looked like a wall of hills on the sea. At first there didn't seem to be any harbor. But then the hills seemed to part, and the *Manatee* moved into a long bay. It was a good harbor, protected on all sides by land. At the end of the bay lay a small beach. Reaching into the harbor from the beach was a stone boat landing.

"We'll tie up here," Ballard said as the *Manatee* neared the landing. "Jump out, Bill, and tie the line."

As they all left the *Manatee*, Gabby started off alone. He saw a dirt road winding from the landing into the hills. He was about to follow it when Ballard called.

"Not that way, Gabby! You had better wait for the rest of us."

Dave Ballard told them all to stay together and follow him. Then he pointed out a trail to their right. The trail followed along the beach for a little way. Then it began to climb sharply up the side of the hill.

"This is the trail the monks built many years ago," Ballard said as they climbed. "At one time it was paved with stone all the way to the top. As you can see, the monks used the beach stones for paving. But many of them have washed away."

As the trail went higher, the steps became wider. The steps, made of heavy blocks of stone, had lasted better than the paving.

"Think of carrying all that rock up this hill!" Vinny said, stopping for breath.

"You wouldn't have made a very good monk, I'm afraid," Bill told his sister. "Here, I'll give you a hand."

After one last turn in the trail they came in sight of the monastery. A long flight of stone steps led from the trail to the ruins.

When they finally reached the top of the steps, they found they were standing in what once had been a court. Like the trail, it, too, was paved with stone.

Little was left of the monastery but parts of the walls. Much of the roof had fallen. The heavy beams that once had carried the roof lay in the ruins.

"Look," Gabby said, pointing across the court. "A road comes right up to the monastery. Isn't that the same road we saw by the landing?"

"You mean we climbed that long trail when we could have come by the road? Oh, no!" said Vinny.

"The road goes through a valley. We took the trail because it's much quicker," Mr. Ballard said. "By way of the road it would take two hours to climb here."

"Oh," Vinny said. "Well, maybe we can go back by the road."

"We'll see," Dave Ballard said. "What's in that basket, Vinny? We all need something to eat after that climb."

Vinny placed the basket on a fallen beam and took out rolls and coffee. After they had finished eating,

43

Ballard led them through the ruins. As they came out of the shadows and into the court again, Vinny looked around.

"Where is Gabby? And Lonnie? Where did they go?" she asked.

Dave Ballard frowned. "You don't suppose they started back by way of the road, do you?"

"There they are, up on the hill behind the ruins," Bill said. He pointed to a line of trees near the top of the hill. The two boys were running toward the trees.

Dave Ballard called to them. "Come back here! Lonnie! Gabby! Hurry up! We have to leave now!"

The two boys stopped. They were looking at something behind the trees. Then they turned to each other. They seemed to be very excited.

Ballard called to them again in a sharp voice. After a few moments the two boys started down the hill.

"I thought I told you not to leave the rest of us," Ballard said when they had returned. "Now stay close to me!"

"But Mr. Ballard," Gabby said, "there's someone up there on the hill."

44

"You're dreaming," Ballard said. "Come on, get your things. We're leaving."

"But there is," Gabby said. "There's a little graveyard up there. We saw some crosses and two big headstones. Someone was behind one of the headstones, watching us. We caught a look at him just before he ducked. He was wearing a kind of hood—a dark hood over his head."

Ballard stared at the two boys. "No," he said finally. "What you saw was a shadow—the shadow of a tree blowing in the wind. Or maybe," he smiled, "a ghost. Isn't every ruin supposed to have a ghost or two?"

Lonnie studied Ballard's face. "Sure, it was all in our heads," he said. "Get your things, genius. Can't you see Mr. Ballard is in a hurry to leave?"

Ballard gave Lonnie a sharp look. Then he picked up Vinny's basket and started down the stone steps.

"Can't we go back by the road?" Vinny asked.

But Dave Ballard didn't turn. One by one, the others fell in line behind him. Bill was last. Before he left the court, he took off his jacket and placed it behind a rock. Then he started after the others.

45

Chapter Five

AN EMPTY POCKET

Dave Ballard led the way down the trail. Now and then he turned to make sure Lonnie and Gabby were following.

"Psst! Vinny," Bill whispered. "I left my jacket at the ruins. If Mr. Ballard should miss me, tell him I went back to get it."

Bill dropped behind as the others went around a sharp turn in the trail. Then he started back toward the monastery. He climbed the long flight of steps and ran through the ruins. He hurried up the hill toward the line of trees.

As he neared them, he could see a row of crosses that stood in the small graveyard on the other side. Together in one corner of the graveyard were the headstones Gabby had seen. Bill stopped in front of them. He could just make out the letters. On one he saw Justin Martineau, 1892–1956; on the other, Joanna Martineau, 1905–1941.

46

With a puzzled frown, Bill turned and walked down the hill. Passing through the ruins once more, he stopped to get his jacket. As he started to pick it up, something about it seemed different. Of course! He had rolled up the jacket and placed it behind the rock. Now it lay across the rock as if it had been dropped there.

Suddenly Bill heard a sound from the ruins, as if something had brushed against a wall. From somewhere in the shadows came another sound, that of a stone falling on stone. Bill heard it roll to a stop. He turned quickly. Looking through an opening in the wall, he thought he saw something move.

"Anyone there?" he called out.

There was no answer. Bill knew there was not enough time to search the ruins. The others were surely near the end of the trail by this time. Mr. Ballard was cross, and there was no use making him more angry. Picking up the jacket, Bill slipped it on and hurried down the stone steps. Out of breath, he caught up with the others at the end of the winding trail.

"You were never even missed," Vinny whispered. "Mr. Ballard was keeping his eye on the boys. Did you see anything interesting?"

Bill nodded. There was no time to tell Vinny more. They were nearing the landing, and Ballard was climbing on board the *Manatee*. Bill waited until the others were all on the boat. Then he picked up the line and jumped on board, too.

Mr. Ballard no longer seemed to be angry at Lonnie and Gabby. He was smiling again as they headed out of the small harbor.

"Well? What did you think of Monks' Island and the monastery?" he asked. "Have you seen enough of its ruins for now?"

"I think I've had enough climbing to last me a year," Vinny answered. "But the ruins were really interesting."

"And seeing that *ghost* just made the day," Lonnie said.

Mr. Ballard turned away as though he had not heard. Vinny frowned at Lonnie and shook her head. Lonnie kept still for the rest of the ride.

50

It was a little before one when they reached Morgan's Landing. Bill helped Mr. Ballard tie up the *Manatee*. They thanked Mr. Ballard for the ride and left the landing.

As the four drove home in the hearse, Bill told the others about the two headstones.

"I can't figure it out," he said. "Someone had to mark those two headstones and put them in place. Joanna died in 1941 and Justin in 1956. If Paul was ten in 1941, he must have run away before 1950—no later. So who made the headstones?"

"Could Mr. Ballard have marked them?" Gabby asked.

"No," answered Vinny. "Mr. Ballard didn't come to Morgan Bay until long after the Martineaus were dead. He has been here only four years."

"But why doesn't he want us to find out about the Martineaus?" Gabby asked. "He tried to tell us Miss Lucy was wrong about a house being on Monks' Island. Then he wouldn't let us near that dirt road. Say! I think I know why. We would have seen the house from the road."

51

"There's a lot we might have seen if we had explored Monks' Island alone," Bill said. "I'm sure, now, that's why Mr. Ballard finally decided to take us there."

Lonnie had a knowing look on his face, but he said nothing.

Once home the four of them headed for the kitchen. Vinny made some sandwiches and then sat down with the telephone book.

"What are you looking for in the telephone book?" Lonnie asked. "Kenneth Martin's name? Man, I never thought of that!"

"Shh! We may find out something," Vinny said as she picked up the telephone and placed a call.

"Doctor Cook? This is Vinny Summers. We came to see you yesterday. Yes. . . . That's right, about Kenneth Martin. May I ask you one more thing? Do you remember a boy named Paul Martineau?"

Vinny nodded to the others as Doctor Cook answered. Then she asked, "Could that photograph we have be a picture of him? . . . Of course, I understand. . . . Yes, thank you very much. We will."

Putting down the telephone, Vinny turned to Lonnie. "Doctor Cook remembers the name Martineau, but he says he never saw Paul after he graduated. That was a long time ago. He would like to see the photograph again. He wants to check it with Paul's picture at the academy."

"You mean—Doctor Cook thinks that my dad and Paul Martineau were the same man?" Lonnie said slowly.

"He doesn't want to say until he has seen the pictures together," Vinny answered. "Why don't we take your photograph over now?"

"Where is it? You had it yesterday, Vinny."

"When I came home from Miss White's, I put it in the pocket of your jacket, the one with the zipper."

Lonnie looked in his pockets and frowned. "Oh, I remember now. I was wearing Bill's jacket yesterday. That's where it is."

"It was the dark jacket on the hall table," said Vinny. "Of course, Bill is wearing it now."

"This one? But the pockets are empty," Bill said. "Are you sure it was this jacket? Did you close the zipper?"

"I'm sure of it. I clearly remember closing the zipper of that pocket."

Lonnie looked from one to the other, his face white.

Bill sat down at the table, closed his eyes, and put his head in his hands.

"Wait a minute—wait a minute," he said. "I didn't use that zipper pocket all day. But look, it's open!"

Bill told them about coming back from the graveyard and finding his jacket on the rock. "There was someone in those ruins. I'm sure of it now. And that's who took the photograph. The picture couldn't have slipped out of the pocket with the zipper closed. And it couldn't have been taken any other time because that was the only time I was not wearing the jacket."

"It must have been that guy with the hood—the one Ballard called a ghost. Why, the . . ." Lonnie slammed the table with his hand. "He figured he might find

54

something in the jacket. He emptied its pockets and then he heard Bill coming, so he dropped the jacket and ran."

"I think that's just what happened, Lonnie," Bill said. "But how are we going to get that picture back again? We need it to take to Doctor Cook."

"That 'ghost' wouldn't have any use for that picture," Gabby said. "Maybe he just dropped it in the ruins."

"We have to get back to Monks' Island right away," Lonnie said. "And this time we won't have Mr. Dave Ballard on our trail!"

Chapter Six

CAUGHT!

"It's not quite two," Bill said, looking at his watch. "There's still enough time to get to the island and back. Let's try to get a ride."

The four of them piled into the old hearse again. In a few minutes they drove through the gate of the club.

"The rest of you wait here," Bill said, pulling the hearse to a stop. "I'll see if Mr. Ballard is still around. He might guess something is up if he sees the four of us here again."

Bill soon returned with good news. "Mr. Ballard left the club half an hour ago," he said. "And I found a ride for us. Some friends know the captain of one of the fishing boats out on the bay. They will row us out to the *Harbor Bee*, and Captain Miles will drop us at the island."

"You mean the *Harbor Bee* is going to leave us on Monks' Island? How will we get home again?" Vinny asked as they hurried to the boat landing.

"Captain Miles can pick us up at ten tonight on his way back," Bill said. "I'm sorry I couldn't work out a better way. Do you think we should wait until tomorrow?"

"Not on your life!" Lonnie said. "I'll walk all the way before I'll wait until tomorrow."

Bill's friends rowed them out to Captain Miles' fishing boat. One by one, Vinny and the boys climbed on board. They called their thanks to Bill's friends as they rowed away.

As the *Harbor Bee* started for Monks' Island, the wind began to blow. Suddenly Gabby pointed across the bay.

"Say, look at those clouds. It looks as if a storm is coming."

Bill nodded. "I hope we won't have any trouble getting back to Morgan's Landing. It's getting darker by the minute."

Soon the fishing boat reached Monks' Island. Protected by the hills, the little harbor was still calm. Captain Miles let Lonnie and the Summers off at the old stone landing.

"Be here at ten tonight," he told them. "I'll try to come back for you. But if a storm comes up, the Coast Guard will ask me to wait at Box Island Harbor until it blows over."

"Do you think there will be a storm?" Bill asked, looking up at the clouds.

"There will be for sure if the wind turns," Miles answered. "But I guess you have a place to stay tonight if I can't come for you."

There was no point in telling Captain Miles they had no place to stay. Miles was on his way to Box Island. They couldn't ask him to take them back to Morgan's Landing. If the storm came, they would just have to take cover somewhere and wait. They thanked the captain for the ride and watched the fishing boat leave the harbor.

Lonnie's only thought was to return to the ruins as quickly as he could. He wanted to find the missing photograph. He was not at all interested in taking the long dirt road to the monastery.

"The monks' trail will be a lot quicker," he said. "After I find the picture, I'll go around by the road."

60

"Really, I think we should stay together," Vinny said. "We'll go with you, Lonnie."

Lonnie shook his head. "That's too much of a climb for you to make again. I'll be all right alone."

"There's only one way to settle this," Bill said. "Gabby, you go with Lonnie. I had better stay with Vinny. The two of us can explore the road."

Vinny finally gave in to Bill and Lonnie. She and her brother watched the two younger boys start up the monks' trail. Then they began walking along the dirt road. It led to the left of the stone landing and began to wind through the hills.

Bill stopped to look at marks in the dry dirt. "This road was used not too long ago. I believe these marks were made by a wagon," he said.

"A wagon! Then someone must live on the island," Vinny said.

"Mr. Ballard might have used the road," Bill said. "Maybe his interest in marine biology is just a front."

"Oh, Bill! A front for what?"

"Smugglers," Bill answered. "Maybe skin diving isn't really why Mr. Ballard comes out here so much. He may be tied in with some smugglers who are bringing contraband to Monks' Island. Mr. Ballard picks it up and takes it to Morgan Bay on the *Manatee*. I can't think of a better place to keep contraband than on an empty island, can you?"

"But Bill," said Vinny. "Mr. Ballard comes to the islands to study sea life."

"That's what he says," Bill answered. "Remember what Miss Wellington told us. Smugglers used to keep contraband on this island long ago."

"Yes," Vinny said. "A *long time ago*! You sure have that figured out, genius. I hope you have figured out where we're going to stay tonight. A drop of rain just hit me. And look at those clouds piling up over the hills."

Suddenly a crash of thunder shook the clouds, and a shower of rain hit the road. Bill and Vinny broke into a run. The road made a sharp turn, and a small valley came into sight. It lay in the middle of the island, protected by the hills.

"There it is, Vinny, the Martineau place," Bill said, pointing through the rain.

Half way across the small valley, they saw what looked like a row of trees. Over the top of the trees, they could see the dark roof of a house. Near that stood a stone barn. Out in the field, they saw a horse.

"Let's take cover in that barn," Vinny said. "I hope the boys reached the ruins in time to get out of this rain."

They hurried on and soon came to a crossing in the road. To the right near the top of the hill lay the ruins; to the left were the barn and house they had seen.

"Come on," Bill said, pulling Vinny after him as they passed the row of trees.

The barn door was standing wide open. A freezing wind followed the two as they ran inside. Standing in the middle of the barn was an old wagon. Along one wall were empty stalls. Bill and Vinny slipped into one of the stalls and sat down to get their breath.

"I'm freezing," Vinny said, pulling her jacket around her. "Do you suppose we could close that big door?"

Bill left the stall and went to the door. He looked through the rain at the Martineau house. He didn't see anyone around. The windows seemed dark and empty. Bill carefully closed the barn door.

"I'm not sure about that place," he said to his sister. "It seems to be empty. But still it looks as though someone has been keeping it up."

Bill checked the wagon standing in the middle of the barn. "This wagon is quite old, but it still works," he said. "And look at the marks on the floor. They look like the ones near the harbor."

Bill walked on through the barn, looking in each of the empty stalls. Finding nothing of interest in the stalls, he sat down beside his sister.

"Find any contraband?" Vinny asked.

Bill shook his head. "I'm afraid not. If the Martineau place is a base for smugglers, they are not keeping their contraband in this barn."

"I still can't see Dave Ballard as a smuggler," Vinny said.

"You're right, Vinny. I guess I was just carried away with the idea."

"I wonder if that house is really empty," said Vinny. "If we could get inside, we could make a fire and dry our clothes. We'll freeze if we have to stay in this barn all night."

"You're right. There's no use staying here if we don't have to," Bill said.

They opened the barn door and stepped out into a dark night. Suddenly something moved toward them. For a moment they stood staring through the rain.

"Oh, it's only an old horse," Bill said. "Come on."

Bill and Vinny faced the blowing rain and ran to the long porch. The horse followed after them. Bill put his head against the front door, but he heard nothing. No one was in the house.

"Bill!" Vinny cried suddenly. "Someone is coming.

Look! Isn't that a light over there by the trees? There's a man walking down the road."

"Quick, duck out of sight," Bill said, pulling Vinny along the dark porch to the corner of the house. From around the corner they watched the light move nearer through the showering rain.

At last the beam of a flashlight fell across the porch. Behind it they could see the tall figure of a man. Bill and Vinny stepped back, holding their breath. A moment later they heard the heavy front door slam. Looking around the corner again, they saw a light beaming through the window.

Together they slipped back along the porch to look in the window. Bill had just caught sight of the man inside when there was a crash! Vinny had fallen over a rocking chair on the porch. As Bill turned to help her, the door opened.

"Who is out there?" a man's voice called.

The voice was Dave Ballard's.

Chapter Seven

THUNDER OVER THE MONASTERY

Lonnie and Gabby were in sight of the monastery when the wind suddenly changed. It came at them, blowing around the hill from the sea. Minutes later they heard the crash of thunder. Just as the rain started, the boys reached the last flight of steps at the end of the trail.

Running up the steps, they ducked into the ruins. There was little cover in the old monastery. Rain fell through the broken roof, and every roll of thunder was followed by the sound of falling stones.

"We had better find the picture and get out of here," Lonnie said. "This place could fall down any minute."

"Well, stop talking and start looking," Gabby said.

They picked their way across the fallen beams and through the ruined halls. Though little of the roof was left, the storm clouds above gave no light. The shadows became darker and darker. The boys passed from one room to the next, searching the stone floors.

69

"I don't see a thing, Lonnie," Gabby finally said. "Maybe the man didn't drop the picture. Maybe he kept it."

"Don't say that. It's here somewhere. We must be blind, that's all."

"We have searched every part of this place," Gabby told him.

"Then we'll go over every step of it again," Lonnie said. "This time let's start from the court."

With a sigh Gabby pulled his jacket over his head to protect him from the rain. Then he followed Lonnie to the paved court.

"This is where we were all standing just before we left. Mr. Ballard picked up the basket and started down the steps," Lonnie said. "Bill was taking off his jacket. He must have put it down about here."

"I get it," Gabby answered. "When Bill came back for the jacket, the other guy must have slipped into that middle hall. But we have looked in there."

Lonnie stepped from the court into the hall again. "Look at those," he said, pointing to a pile of stones. "I don't remember seeing those when we came through

70

here with Mr. Ballard. They must have fallen and blocked the door to one of the rooms. And that's one room we didn't search."

"How can we? We're not going to move all those rocks, are we?" Gabby said, frowning.

Lonnie went back to the court. He walked along the wall a few steps and called to Gabby. "Here is an opening. I think if we climb through it, we'll be inside that room."

As he talked, Lonnie was stepping through the small opening. Then he slipped his head inside.

Suddenly Lonnie cried out in alarm. "Here he is, Gabby! The guy is in here. Come quick!"

Lonnie slipped through the opening, and Gabby climbed after him. There on the floor lay a man caught by the fallen stones. The figure was face down, its head covered by a dark hood. Beside him lay the missing photograph.

"Maybe he's dead," Lonnie whispered.

"No," Gabby said, pulling away the man's hood. "I don't think so."

In the dark shadows Gabby could see little of the face but dark eyebrows. Lonnie began to pull away the stones. The man made a sound and tried to move.

"Careful now," Gabby said. "We'll have you out of here in a minute."

Another roll of thunder shook the ruins. Just in time, Gabby and Lonnie pulled the man away from the wall. With a crash another part of the wall gave way and sent rocks rolling across the room.

"This place is falling in!" Lonnie said. "Man, how are we going to get out of here with that door blocked?"

"We'll climb through the wall the way we came in," Gabby said.

"With him?" Lonnie said, nodding toward the man. "Are you kidding? It's not wide enough. The two of us might be able to carry him, but we'll never be able to get him through that opening. We might hurt him."

"We had better go for help," Gabby said. "We'll have to try and find Vinny and Bill."

"You go," Lonnie said. "I'll stay. We can't leave him here alone."

"But—but—what if the walls . . ."

"Go *on*," Lonnie said in an angry voice. "Run!"

Gabby slipped through the opening and out into the rain again. He ran across the clearing, slipping on the stone paving. Running through the gate, he started down the road. Night had fallen, and he could not see very far in front of him. With every crash of thunder, Gabby thought of the two in the falling ruins.

All at once, off to his right he saw a beam of light. It seemed to be moving. Gabby decided it would be quicker to go across the open field. He stepped from the road. Suddenly he fell down a hill and rolled to a stop near a pile of rocks.

"Boy, what a genius you are," he said as he caught his breath. "You should never have left the road."

But the hill behind Gabby was too high to climb. There was nothing to do but go across the field. He raced on. Before long he reached a big, dark barn. Behind that was the lighted window of a house. Jumping the steps, Gabby fell across the porch.

Dave Ballard, the rain still running off his clothes, opened the door. He caught Gabby by the hand, pulled him into the room, and slammed the door. Behind Mr. Ballard stood Vinny and Bill.

"Well, now, is this all? Or are there more coming?" Ballard asked in a sharp voice. "Where is Lonnie?"

"Up at—up at the ruins," Gabby said. "You have to help them. They—the wall fell in and blocked the door. The man is hurt. We couldn't get him out . . ."

"What man?" Ballard cried in alarm.

"I don't know—that man—the ghost. Bring a light and come on!"

"Paul Martineau," Ballard said. "I'll get blankets. Bill, light these lanterns. How was he hurt, Gabby?"

Quickly Gabby told Ballard how they had found Paul Martineau. "I guess he was hit by falling rocks."

"We can't take the wagon, it will slip on the road,"

76

Ballard said. "We'll take the horse. You ride him, Gabby. You need the rest. Hurry, kids."

As they started off, the heavy wind stopped blowing. The storm had passed, and only a light shower was falling.

"I asked Paul not to stay alone on this island," Ballard said. "I've been afraid something like this would happen to him."

"How do you happen to know Paul Martineau?" Vinny asked.

"I knew him in Korea. We were at the same base. Paul was hurt and sent back to this country," Ballard answered. "I didn't run into him again until I started teaching in Morgan Bay. I was skin diving out here one day and decided to explore the island. I found Paul living here.

"He had spent two years with the doctors. They had put what was left of him back together again. I guess they did all that anyone could. But he won't leave Monks' Island. He won't see anyone, not even old friends. I think I'm the only one who knows he's here. That's the way Paul wants it."

"And you have been trying to protect him all this time?" Vinny's voice was very kind.

Ballard went on. "I saw the hearse in back of the club. I had an idea you had come back here. I knew I had to follow you. I wanted to find some way to keep you away from Paul."

Now they were near the top of the hill and the ruins. As quickly as he could, Bill told Ballard about Lonnie, about the Home, the photograph, and Lonnie's search for his island.

"Just hope we're in time!" Ballard said. "There's the gate. Run!"

Chapter Eight

THE GHOST TALKS

"Lonnie? Are you still there? Are you all right?"

Dave Ballard placed a lantern in the opening of the wall. In its beam he saw the small room piled with stones. Against the back wall sat Lonnie, holding Paul Martineau's head.

"Man, am I happy to see you—and I mean happy. This ghost is getting heavy, and we're freezing."

Ballard put the lantern on the floor and climbed into the room. In a moment he was beside the still figure of Paul Martineau. He saw that the jacket covering the man was Lonnie's.

"Put this on, Lonnie," Dave Ballard said, taking the jacket from Martineau. "Vinny, hand me those blankets."

By the light of his lantern, Bill studied the small opening in the wall.

"I believe if this opening were wider, we could carry Mr. Martineau through here," he told Ballard. "I don't think it would take long to pull out these stones."

Ballard nodded. "Good idea, but be careful."

Paul Martineau's eyes opened. He frowned and closed them again.

"He's coming out of it," Lonnie said to Ballard.

"Dave? Is that you?" Paul Martineau whispered.

"Yes, Paul. You are going to be all right. We'll have you home soon," Ballard said.

Vinny, Gabby, and Bill finally pulled out enough stones in the opening of the wall. Martineau, rolled in a blanket, was carried out. Ballard climbed on the back of the waiting horse.

"Careful, boys," he said. "I'll hold Paul up here in front of me."

With Ballard holding Paul Martineau on the old horse, they started slowly down the hill. The rain had stopped; the clouds had moved on.

"Man! Look at that valley!" Lonnie whispered to Vinny. "I think I'm walking through the middle of a dream."

They passed the row of trees and soon reached the house. Once inside, they built a fire and made a place near it for Paul Martineau. Dave Ballard covered him with blankets.

"He will rest for the night," Dave said. "You can talk to him tomorrow."

Then Dave Ballard led the Summers and Lonnie through the old house.

"There has been nothing new in this house for a hundred years," Ballard smiled. "The only light is from lanterns. The table and chairs in the kitchen were made by hand. Nearly all that Paul eats can be found here on the island. He cooks over the open fire."

"Man, what a life! This must be like the old days," Lonnie said.

Ballard told the boys where to wash up. "Come on," he said to Vinny. "Let's see if we can find some dry clothes and something for dinner. Then we'll all try to rest. You can explore more tomorrow."

Day was beaming through the window when Vinny opened her eyes. From the kitchen came the sound of voices. Vinny called to the boys to get up. Hurrying down, they found Paul Martineau and Dave Ballard having coffee by the fire.

"Here they are, Paul—Vinny, Bill, and Gabby Summers and Lonnie Martin. Yesterday I was so angry at them! But if they had not come back . . ."

"I wouldn't be here," Paul Martineau finished as he shook hands with each of them. He didn't let go of Lonnie's hand but pulled him closer. Suddenly he reached up and brushed back the boy's long hair. He began to smile.

"He has the Martineau eyebrows, all right. So this is Kenneth's boy."

"Martineau eyebrows!" Lonnie said. "What do you mean?"

"Dave told me that your father was Kenneth Martin. Kenneth's father and my dad were brothers. But Kenneth's dad left the island as a young man and settled near Jethro. He changed his name to Martin by dropping the 'eau' letters."

84

Lonnie stared at him. "Then you and my dad were cousins?" he finally said.

"Yes, we were cousins," Paul Martineau said. "But we were really more like brothers. Kenneth used to come to see me at the academy. And he spent every summer on Monks' Island. He liked it here. I'm afraid I couldn't think of anything but getting away from the island in those days.

"I wanted to do something exciting. And I could think of nothing more exciting than being a flyer in the war. I talked Kenneth into going with me to flight school. I didn't pass, but Kenneth finished and became a flyer. Later, in a letter, he said that he was thinking of getting married. I never heard from him again. His folks were dead by the time I returned to this country. No one could tell me what had happened to him."

"He was shot down in the Korean War," Lonnie said. "He died before I was born."

"Kenneth was a good boy and a good man," Paul Martineau said. "He might have come back if it had not been for me."

Lonnie walked to the window, his hands in his pockets, and stood staring across the fields.

"Oh no," he said finally. "A lot of people didn't come back, and they were not all flyers. My dad didn't die because he was a flyer; he died because he was in a war."

"Lonnie is right, Paul," Ballard said kindly. "But you have not told us what happened at the ruins yesterday."

Paul Martineau brushed his hand across his eyebrows and frowned. "I remember walking up the hill toward the graveyard. I was going to check on the bees. That's why I had that hood over my head. It protects me from the bees." He smiled. "I never dreamed I would be taken for a ghost. I heard voices so I walked over the hill and saw two boys running toward the graveyard. I ducked out of sight. I didn't know who you people were or that Dave was with you.

"I had not been to the ruins in years," Martineau went on. "Kenneth and I went there sometimes when we were young. So when I thought you had left, I decided to explore the monastery again.

86

"There was a jacket someone had left behind. I looked through the pockets for something that might tell me who owned it. I had the photograph half out of the pocket when I heard steps.

"I dropped the jacket and ducked into the ruins until Bill left. Then I looked at the photograph in my hand and saw Kenneth's face. I started after Bill and —well, that's all I remember."

"You must have fallen against that wall," Ballard said. "I've been afraid something like this would happen, and there would be no one to help you, Paul."

Paul Martineau shook his head slowly. "I know, Dave," he said. "I guess I've been trying to think that I didn't need help. But all along, you have been helping me. You have kept coming out here, bringing things I needed."

Dave Ballard frowned. "You don't need help, Paul. But living alone in a town and living alone on an island are two different things."

Paul Martineau stood beside Lonnie at the window. "What would you think of living here?" he asked the boy. "Would you miss having friends around?"

87

"You mean, you want me to stay?"

"Well, we're the last of the Martineaus, Lonnie. I figure you and I own Monks' Island together. It will be all yours one day. In the fall, of course, you will have to go to high school. But in the summer we can..."

"Shoot! I dropped out of school," Lonnie broke in. "I could just stay out here all the time."

"I think Kenneth would have wanted his son to finish school," Paul Martineau said kindly.

Lonnie shook his head and frowned. "I couldn't go back now. I would be way behind the other kids."

"I can help you to make up the work," Dave said. "I can bring the books, and Paul and I will teach you. When school opens, you will think differently about going back. Paul, now that Lonnie's here, why not do something about that dream of yours?"

"You mean putting this land to work?" Paul said. "Oh, that was just a wild dream, I'm afraid."

"Don't let that stop you. The wilder, the better!" Lonnie said. With a wide smile he looked over at Vinny, Bill, and Gabby. "I had a wild dream once," he finished, "and look what happened!"

EXERCISES

Chapter One

THE BOY WITH THE SWITCHBLADE

Was It or Wasn't It?

Some of the sentences below tell about things that happened in the story and some do not. On your paper write each sentence that does not belong in the story.

1. "Well!" Vinny said, "I'm afraid Mother and Dad took their switchblade."
2. Gabby had gone to the dump to shoot rats.
3. Gabby handed Bill a broken slingshot.
4. All of the boys in the club called the Shadows owned rats.
5. Gabby told Vinny and Bill that Lonnie was living in a box at the dump.
6. Lonnie needed the slingshot and ball bearings to shoot something to eat.
7. Bill and Gabby climbed into the hearse and drove to Monks' Island.
8. Gabby knew he had found Lonnie's box because his blanket was in it.
9. Lonnie was shooting ball bearings at the blanket.
10. Bill and Gabby ducked down behind the box.
11. Gabby and Bill asked Lonnie to come and eat dinner at their house.
12. "I'll say one thing for Lonnie," Bill said. "He has long hair."
13. Vinny was cooking sandwiches for dinner.
14. "Man, I really like this house," Lonnie said, looking slowly around the kitchen.
15. Lonnie only stared at his dinner, frowning.
16. "I never eat fish because the police don't want me to," said Lonnie.

WHICH WORD DOES NOT BELONG?

Number your paper from 1 to 8. After each number write the one word on the line that does not belong with the others.

1. fish   hearse   sandwiches
2. box   switchblade   slingshot
3. boxes   cans   islands
4. hair   eyebrows   shower
5. calm   alarmed   excited
6. block   dark   mile
7. door   knife   porch
8. shoot   climb   anyone

TO THINK ABOUT AND TALK ABOUT

1. In the place where you live, is it all right to carry a slingshot? A switchblade? Any other kind of knife?
2. When Gabby found Lonnie living at the dump, he thought of taking him sandwiches. Vinny thought of having Lonnie come to dinner. What would you have done and why?

SEARCH FOR AN ISLAND

WHO IS WHO?

Number your paper from 1 to 19. After each number put the name of the person the sentence tells about.

1. He never forgot a face.
2. He had a picture of Kenneth Martin.
3. He moved away from Jethro.
4. He lost his mom and dad.
5. He saw his horse in a field.
6. He lived on an island.
7. He dreamed about an island.
8. He took pictures for the high schools.
9. He had a kind face.
10. He didn't find Kenneth Martin's name in his book of graduates.
11. His name was on a door.
12. He ran away from a Home.
13. He was head of a boarding school.
14. He was shot down in Korea.
15. She kept a letter.
16. He reached into the desk behind him and pulled out a map.
17. She didn't think there was any hope.
18. His name was on the back of a photograph.
19. He had white hair.

TO THINK ABOUT AND TALK ABOUT

What made Lonnie and the Summers go to Jethro to find out about Kenneth Martin? At what other places might they have found out if Martin had ever lived in Jethro? Where would you have looked?

Chapter Three

DEAD END

Choose the right ending for each of the sentences below.

1. Lonnie wanted to give up the search for his father because
   (a) he was a genius.
   (b) it seemed to be a wild idea.
   (c) the hearse stalled.
   (d) he wanted to take a shower.
2. Marine biology is the study of
   (a) high school teachers.
   (b) skin divers.
   (c) sea life.
   (d) islands.
3. There was a Coast Guard base at
   (a) Morgan Bay.
   (b) Monks' Island.
   (c) Box Island.
   (d) Table Rock Island.
4. Vinny wanted to talk to Miss Wellington because
   (a) she owned Monks' Island.
   (b) she would know if anyone had lived on Monks' Island.
   (c) her son was a Frenchman.
   (d) she knew lots of smugglers.
5. The island had been settled by monks who
   (a) became smugglers.
   (b) drove away the Indians.
   (c) built a barn made of stone.
   (d) built a small monastery.

93

6. When the monastery fell into ruins,
   (a) Miss Lucy began to cry.
   (b) a Frenchman settled on Monks' Island.
   (c) the smugglers moved to Morgan Bay.
   (d) the Coast Guard took the monks away.
7. Joanna Martineau died when
   (a) the boat went down.
   (b) her son was ten years old.
   (c) her son ran away.
   (d) her husband was away in Morgan Bay.
8. Bill was puzzled because Mr. Ballard had
   (a) not told them all about the island.
   (b) not told them about May White.
   (c) left on the *Manatee*.
   (d) sent them to Lucy Wellington.
9. May White told Vinny that Paul Martineau
   (a) couldn't wait to get home to Monks' Island.
   (b) had dropped out of the Jethro Academy.
   (c) dreamed of being a teacher.
   (d) had gone to boarding school.

Chapter Four

OF RUINS AND SHADOWS

FIND THE RIGHT WORD

Choose the right ending for each sentence.

1. To get the meaning of something is to _____.
   (understand) (dream) (decide) (frown)
2. A place where monks live together is called a _____.
   (club) (monastery) (ruin) (hotel)
3. A very old building of which only some parts are left is called a _____.
   (manor) (monastery) (ruin) (court)
4. Big boards used to hold up a roof are called _____.
   (zippers) (walls) (bearings) (beams)
5. A place with no roof but with walls around it is called a _____.
   (court) (harbor) (ruin) (monastery)
6. Something for which it is hard to find an answer may be called a _____.
   (storm) (shadow) (puzzle) (ruin)
7. A stone used to mark a grave is called a _____.
   (beach stone) (paving stone) (cross) (headstone)
8. A covering for the head is called a _____.
   (basket) (hood) (pocket) (slip)
9. Land with water all around it is called _____.
   (a bay) (a landing) (an island) (a valley)

TO THINK ABOUT AND TALK ABOUT

Do you think Lonnie was right when he said that you have to like someone before you can understand him? Or do you think you must understand someone before you can like him?

Chapter Five

AN EMPTY POCKET

Number your paper from 1 to 15. After each number put a T if the sentence is right, or an N if the sentence is not right.

1. Mr. Ballard left his jacket at the monastery.
2. Justin and Joanna Martineau's headstones were in the graveyard.
3. Bill did not search the ruins because he didn't want to make Mr. Ballard cross.
4. Bill was not missed because the boys were keeping an eye on Mr. Ballard.
5. Lonnie believed that he had seen a ghost at the ruins.
6. Bill could not understand who had made the headstones because no one lived on the island after the Martineaus died.
7. Vinny thought Mr. Ballard had made the headstones.
8. Mr. Ballard wanted the Summers and Lonnie to see everything on Monks' Island.
9. Dr. Cook remembered Paul Martineau's name.
10. Dr. Cook wanted to check the telephone book for Kenneth Martin's name.
11. Vinny had put the photograph of Kenneth Martin in the jacket on the hall table.
12. The jacket with the photograph in the pocket was the one Lonnie had on at the ruins.
13. Bill was sure someone at the ruins had taken the photograph from the jacket pocket.
14. Lonnie thought Mr. Ballard had taken the photograph.
15. Lonnie and the Summers wanted to go back to Monks' Island on Mr. Ballard's boat.

96

Chapter Six
CAUGHT!

Number your paper from 1 to 15. After each number write the word or words that belong in the sentence.

1. Bill could not get them a ride _____ until late that night.
   (to the island)   (home)   (to the fishing boat)
2. Lonnie and the Summers took _____ to get out to the *Harbor Bee*.
   (the hearse)   (the *Manatee*)   (a row boat)
3. Gabby pointed across the bay and said, "It looks as if _____ is coming."
   (a cloud)   (Dave Ballard)   (a storm)   (Captain Miles)
4. Captain Miles said he would pick them up at _____ at ten if it were not storming.
   (Box Island Harbor)   (Morgan Bay)   (the boat landing)
5. Lonnie's only thought was to find the _____ as soon as he could.
   (ghost)   (photograph)   (ruins)   (landing)
6. Lonnie and Gabby took the _____ to the monastery.
   (monks' trail)   (dirt road)   (photograph)   (wagon)
7. Bill was sure the old road had been used because he found _____.
   (a wagon)   (stone steps)   (smugglers)   (marks)
8. Bill thought the island was being used by smugglers as a place to keep _____.
   (contraband)   (Mr. Ballard)   (wagons)   (skin divers)
9. Around a sharp turn in the road, Bill and Vinny finally saw _____.
   (Lonnie and Gabby)   (clouds)   (the Martineau place)

97

10. Standing in the middle of the barn was _____.
    (an old smuggler)   (a stall)   (some contraband)   (an old wagon)
11. Bill was not sure the _____ was empty.
    (Martineau house)   (stall)   (barn)   (wagon)
12. Vinny wanted to get into the house because she was afraid _____.
    (of the ghost)   (the barn would blow down)   (they would freeze)
13. As they started through the rain toward the house, a _____ came toward them.
    (smuggler)   (horse)   (ghost)   (duck)
14. There was a crash as Vinny fell over _____.
    (the porch)   (the horse)   (the chair)   (the man)
15. The man in the Martineau house was _____.
    (Captain Miles)   (Mr. Martineau)   (Dave Ballard)

Chapter Seven
THUNDER OVER THE MONASTERY

Was It or Wasn't It?

Some of the sentences below tell about things that happened in the story, and some do not. On your paper copy each sentence that belongs in the story. Write the sentences in the order in which they happened.

1. Gabby got on the horse and went as quickly as he could to find Bill.
2. Searching for help, Gabby saw a light and ran toward it.
3. Ballard told the Summers about Paul Martineau as they hurried toward the ruins.
4. Paul Martineau and Dave Ballard had been friends at the Jethro Academy.
5. Lonnie and Gabby ducked into the ruins to get out of the rain.
6. Lonnie and Gabby found the man with the hood over his head.
7. "Thanks for stopping by," said the ghost.
8. The boys found a pile of stones that was blocking one of the rooms.
9. Lonnie went with Gabby to find Vinny and Bill.
10. The two boys saw the missing photograph in the court.
11. The two boys pulled the hurt man away from the wall just as more rocks rolled across the room.
12. Gabby jumped the steps and fell across the porch.
13. Taking lanterns and blankets, Ballard and the Summers went to the monastery.
14. They brought Paul Martineau back in a wagon.
15. "Paul Martineau is no friend of mine," Dave Ballard said.

To Think About and Talk About

Lonnie had been angry at the hooded man for taking his father's photograph. But when he found the man hurt in the ruins, Lonnie stayed with him. Why did he do this? Do you think Lonnie's feelings towards the man had changed? Or do you think he stayed because it was "the right thing to do"? Do you think Lonnie has changed since the beginning of the book? Why?

Chapter Eight

THE GHOST TALKS

Who Is Who?

Number your paper from 1 to 13. After each number write the name of the person that answers the question.

1. Who thought of making the opening in the wall wider by taking out some of the stones?
2. Who was wrapped in blankets?
3. Who rode with Mr. Ballard on the horse?
4. Who thought he was walking through the middle of a dream?
5. Who cooked over an open fire?
6. Who said, "This must be like the old days?"
7. Who had been angry at Lonnie and the Summers?
8. Who was Paul Martineau's cousin?
9. Who talked Kenneth into going to flight school?
10. Who had taken the photograph from the pocket of Bill's jacket?
11. Who had been helping Paul Martineau when he was alone on the island?
12. Who told Lonnie he would help him make up his school work?
13. Whom did Paul Martineau ask to stay with him on Monks' Island?

To Think About and Talk About

1. Which of the people in *The Mystery of Monks' Island* would you rather be?
2. How did you feel about the ending of the story? Would you have liked it better if the "ghost" had turned out to be Kenneth Martin?

101

3. Dave Ballard knew that Paul Martineau didn't want to see anyone. At the same time, Dave thought Martineau should not have been living alone on the island. In Ballard's place, what would you have done? Would you have kept still and protected Paul Martineau? Or would you have tried to make him see people or move from the island? Why?
4. As a boy, Paul Martineau had not liked living on Monks' Island. Do you think his feelings toward the island changed after he came back from the war? If so, what might have happened that changed them?
5. In the beginning do you think Lonnie really believed he would find his island? Or was he just running away from a life he didn't like?

WORD LIST

Running words in *The Mystery of Monks' Island*, the sixth book of the MORGAN BAY MYSTERIES, total 11,322. The number of different words used is 536. The entire vocabulary is listed below. Following each word is the number of the page on which it first appears.

Of the 536 words listed, 478 should be familiar to children reading at third-grade level. The remaining 58 (italicized in the list below) are enrichment words, necessary to the color and context of the story. The 384 starred words were introduced in the first five books of the series.

*a	2	*ask	1	*biology*	23	careful	10
able	12	*at	1	blanket	5	*carry	2
*about	2	*away	1	*blind*	19	*caught	8
academy	18			block	1	*chair	4
*across	5	*back	3	*blow	45	*change	9
*afraid	17	Ballard	22	*board	4	*check	16
*after	5	*ball bearings*	2	*boat	18	clear	12
*again	4	barn	29	*book	19	*climb	4
against	35	*base*	16	born	11	*close	16
ago	29	basket	39	*box	3	*clothes	9
alarm	1	*bay*	4	*boy	1	clouds	57
*all	2	*be	1	breath	35	*club	2
*alone	39	*beach	28	bring	3	*Coast*	
*along	21	*beam*	4	*broke	2	*Guard*	26
*am	3	became	17	*brother	1	*coffee	26
*an	1	because	37	brushed	10	*come	1
*and	1	bee	56	built	23	*contraband*	29
*angry	5	*been	1	*but	3	cook	9
*another	5	*before	1	*by	12	*corner	5
*answer	2	began	12			*could	16
*any	11	*behind	1	*call	2	*couldn't	19
*anyone	5	*believe	13	*calm*	1	*country	3
*anything	3	*beside	5	*came	2	course	9
*are	1	*better	11	*can	2	court	43
*around	2	*big	23	*can't	3	cousin	17
*as	3	*Bill	1	*captain	56	*cover	1

crash	62	*explore*	13
cross	28	*eye	12
cry	3	*eyebrow*	10

*dad	1	*face	2
*dark	1	*fall	47
Dave	23	*fallen*	43
*day	12	*father	13
*dead	2	fell	29
decide	3	*few	4
*desk	13	field	13
*did	11	*figure*	18
*didn't	1	*finally*	8
*die	10	*find	2
different	3	finish	11
dinner	3	*fire	12
dirt	4	*fish	9
*do	1	*flashlight*	4
*doctor	19	*flight*	16
*doesn't	2	*floor	13
*don't	2	*flyer*	11
*door	1	folks	8
*down	1	*follow	4
dream	13	*for	1
*drop	19	forget	12
*drove	4	*found	2
dry	9	*four	18
duck	5	freeze	39
dump	1	Frenchman	
			29
each	11	*friend	4
*eat	3	*from	2
*empty	5	*front	1
*end	4	*frown*	4
*enough	47		
*even	8	*Gabby	1
*every	13	*gate	1
*excited	22	*gave	2

genius	18	*home	1
*get	1	hood	45
ghost	45	hope	16
*give	22	horse	13
*go	1	*hotel	26
*good	1	*hour	1
graduate	18	*house	1
graveyard	45	*how	11
*guess	8	*hundred	13
guy	2	*hurry	23
		*hurt	9
		*I	1
*had	10	*idea*	4
*hair	10	*if	3
half	26	*I'll	4
*hall	9	*I'm	4
*hand	1	*in	1
*happen	20	Indians	28
*happy	26	*inside	5
harbor	39	*interest	12
*has	3	*into	1
*have	1	*is	2
*he	1	*island*	11
*head	2	*isn't	3
headstones	45	*it	1
*heard	8	*its	8
hearse	4	*it's	1
*heavy	42	I've	29
*help	9		
*her	10	*jacket	4
*here	2	*Jethro	4
he's	3	Joanna	29
*high	17	*jump	1
*hill	18	*just	1
*him	1	Justin	29
*his	1		
hit	5	*keep	11
holding	29	kept	13

104

Kenneth	16	*map*	13	*nothing	27	*puzzle	1

Kenneth 16
*kidding 3
kind 3
kitchen 10
*knew 23
knife 2
*know 2
Korea 11

*land 23
lantern 76
*last 13
*later 4
*lay 4
*leave 4
led 4
*left 13
*let 1
*let's 4
*letter 13
*life 3
*light 8
*like 4
*line 10
*little 2
*live 1
*long 1
Lonnie 2
*look 2
*lot 9
*Lucy 28

*made 29
*make 10
*man 8
Manatee 23
*Manor 30
many 28

map 13
marine 23
*mark 17
*married 13
Martin 2
Martineau 29
*may 18
*maybe 3
*me 2
mean 2
middle 63
*might 8
*miles 4
minute 8
*miss 28
mom 10
*moment 17
monastery 29
monk 26
*more 2
*Morgan 4
*mother 1
*move 18
*Mr. 19
*much 12
*must 3
*my 1

*name 12
near 12
*need 3
*never 12
*new 19
*next 3
*night 2
*no 3
*nodded 3
*not 3

*nothing 27
*now 21

*of 1
*off 4
*oh 2
*old 1
*on 2
*once 5
*one 2
*only 10
*open 13
*or 8
*other 11
*our 8
*out 1
*over 3
own 2

*part 16
*pass 13
Paul 34
paved 42
*people 11
photograph 17
photographer 17
*pick 8
*picture 16
pile 4
*place 3
*pocket 1
*point 5
police 2
*porch 1
*protect 39
*pull 1
*put 5

*puzzle 1
*quick 10
quite 28
*rain 5
*ran 1
rat 3
*reached 9
really 1
*remember 13
rest 42
*return 17
ride 50
*right 3
*road 4
*rock 26
*roll 5
*roof 43
*room 1
row 46
ruin 29
*run 11

*said 1
*same 31
sandwiches 3
*sat 22
*saw 8
*say 1
school 17
*sea 23
search 11
*see 1
*seem 20
*seen 29
*sent 13
settled 12
*shadow 2

sharp	12	*stood	28	*tie	23	*way	8
*she	10	*stop	19	*time	8	*we	3
*shook	2	storm	39	*to	1	wear	9
shoot	1	*study	13	together	2	*well	1
shot	9	*sudden	5	*told	8	*we'll	12
*should	10	*summer	1	tomorrow	3	*Wellington	28
shower	9	*suppose	1	tonight	3	*went	1
*side	4	*sure	4	*too	3	*were	1
*sigh	8	switchblade	1	*took	3	*we're	10
sight	42			*top	38	*what	2
*sister	1	*table	9	*toward	8	*what's	1
skin dive	23	*take	11	*town	4	*when	8
slam	1	*talk	12	trail	42	*where	1
slingshot	1	teach	5	*tree	23	*whispered	5
slip	8	teacher	20	*trouble	10	*white	19
*slowly	10	*telephone	39	*try	4	*who	1
*small	5	*tell	2	*turn	4	*why	3
*smile	10	ten	13	*two	1	*wide	23
*smuggler	29	*than	3			wild	12
*so	8	*thank	9	understand	17	*will	5
*some	3	*that	1	*until	3	*wind	39
*someone	5	*that's	1	*up	1	*window	19
*something	1	*the	1	*us	2	*with	1
sometimes	20	*their	19	*use	13	wonder	3
somewhere	5	*them	5			*won't	17
son	29	*then	3	valley	18	*work	2
*soon	13	*there	2	*very	12	*would	1
*sorry	9	*there's	4	*Vinny	1	*wouldn't	2
*sound	37	these	2	*voice	5	wrong	2
spent	10	*they	4				
stall	64	*thing	1	wagon	61	*year	16
*standing	4	*think	9	*wait	1	*yes	26
stared	1	*this	1	*walk	1	yesterday	39
*start	4	*those	19	*wall	28	*you	1
*stay	2	though	18	*want	1	*young	13
*step	1	*thought	22	*war	11	*your	8
*still	18	*through	1	*was	1	you're	11
stone	29	thunder	62	wash	9		
				*watch	20	zipper	36